Dear Parents, Educators, and Guardians,

Thank you for helping your child dive into this book with us. We believe in the power of books to transport readers to other worlds, expand their horizons, and help them discover cultures and experiences that may differ from their own.

We also believe that books should inspire young readers to imagine a diverse world that includes them, a world where they can see themselves as the heroes of their own stories.

These are our hopes for *all* our readers. So come on. Dive in and explore the world with us!

Best wishes,
Your friends at Lee & Low

DIVE INTO READING!

A Special Goodbye

Henry   Lily   Mei   Pablo   Padma

by Samantha Thornhill

illustrated by Shirley Ng-Benitez

Lee & Low Books Inc. New York

For my parents, Tom & Diana —S. T.
To Lee & Low, readers around the world,
and my family—my heartfelt thanks! —S. N-B.

LEE & LOW BOOKS Inc., 95 Madison Avenue, New York, NY 10016 leeandlow.com
Book design by Charice Silverman
Book production by The Kids at Our House
The illustrations are rendered in watercolor and altered digitally
Manufactured in South Korea by Mirae N
Printed on paper from responsible sources
(hc) 10 9 8 7 6 5 4 3 2 1
(pb) 10 9 8 7 6 5 4 3 2 1
First Edition

Library of Congress Cataloging-in-Publication Data
Names: Thornhill, Samantha, author. | Ng-Benitez, Shirley, illustrator.
Title: A special goodbye / by Samantha Thornhill; illustrated by Shirley Ng-Benitez.
Description: First edition. | New York, NY: Lee & Low Books Inc., 2023.
Series: Confetti kids ; 12 | Audience: Ages 4-7. | Audience: Grades K-1.
Summary: When her parents decide to close the family flower shop, Mei
    finds a special way to say goodbye to their neighbors.
Identifiers: LCCN 2022010136 | ISBN 9781643795102 (hardback)
    ISBN 9781643794983 (paperback) | ISBN 9781643794990 (ebk)
Subjects: CYAC: Farewells—Fiction. | Flowers—Fiction. |
    Florists—Fiction. | Neighbors—Fiction. | LCGFT: Picture books.
Classification: LCC PZ7.T3934 Sp 2023 | DDC [E]—dc23
LC record available at https://lccn.loc.gov/2022010136

Contents

Bad News

One evening Mei's parents shared
some bad news.
"We have to close our shop,"
said Mei's father.

Mei's family owned the
neighborhood flower shop.
Mei knew all their neighbors
because of the store.

But this year fewer people
came in to buy flowers.
Mei's parents couldn't pay
the rent anymore.

Walking home, Mei noticed
other stores and restaurants
were closing too.
The owners couldn't pay
the rent either.

"Can we do something to save
the shop?" asked Mei.
"I don't think so,"
said her mother.
Mei started to cry.

The shop was like a second home to her and her little brother, Ming. Sometimes her friends would visit the shop to help choose flowers for customers.

The next day Mei was sitting outside
with her friends Lily, Pablo, Henry,
and Padma.
Mei was very quiet.

"What's wrong, Mei?" asked Padma. Mei told her friends the sad news about her family's flower shop. "We have to close it in a few weeks," said Mei.

"Oh no!" said Pablo.
"But everyone loves the flower
shop!" said Lily.

"Every weekend my mom buys flowers for our home," said Henry. "I'll miss going to the shop after school," said Padma.

Mei was happy to
have her friends around.
"How can we help?"
asked Henry.

"I'm not sure," said Mei.
"But maybe we could do something
special to say goodbye to the shop."

Closing Day

The day came to close the shop.
Mei thought about how her family
worked so hard every day
at the shop.
Mei felt sad.

"Think about all the joy our flowers gave to people," said Mei's father. Mei wondered if people would remember.

Henry, Padma, Lily, and Pablo
entered the shop.
Even with boxes everywhere,
it felt like old times.

"We're here to say goodbye
to the flower shop," said Lily.
"And to help!" said Henry.
"What wonderful friends you have,
Mei," said her mother.

There was a lot of work to do.
They needed to pack everything
neatly into boxes.
They needed to wash the floors
and windows.

There were still flowers everywhere.

The friends had lots of fun helping.
Pablo told jokes.
Padma danced with a broom.
Henry served snacks and tea.

Mei's friends made sure the last day in the shop was a happy one.

Special Delivery

After a few hours they finished
cleaning and packing.
Mei looked at the pretty flowers
sitting by the door.

"What about the flowers?" asked Mei.
"Kids, you can take some flowers
home," said Mei's mom.
"Thank you!" said Padma.

"But there will still be many flowers left," said Lily.
"Can we give away the rest?"

"We can give them away to our neighbors to make them feel special," said Mei.

Mei and her friends gave flowers
to their family and neighbors.

Mei saw some customers on the street and gave them flowers.

THANK YOU
for your
business!

Some customers remembered
their wedding flowers from the shop.
Another customer remembered
the flowers delivered after her baby
was born.

Mei thought about all the joy
her family's flowers gave people.
It was nice to know the shop
would always be remembered.

☆ **Activity** ☆

🌻 Think about all the stores and places in your neighborhood. Do you have a favorite, and why? Draw a picture of what makes it so special.

🌷 If you could open your own store, what kind of store would you open? What kinds of things would you sell? Draw a picture of you running your imaginary store.

🌻 Mei and her family are going through a big change. How do Mei's friends help support her and her family in the story? Write  about ways that you can support your friends if they're feeling sad or need your help.

Samantha Thornhill is a poet and an author of children's books. As an educator, she has taught poetry to acting students at the Juilliard School and creative writing seminars at the Bronx Academy of Letters. Samantha is a native of the twin-island nation of Trinidad and Tobago and lives in Brooklyn, NY. You can learn more about her at samanthaspeaks.com.

Shirley Ng-Benitez loves to draw and write. She creates her art with watercolor, gouache, pencil, and digital techniques. She lives in the Bay Area of California and is inspired by nature, her family, her pup, and two kittens. Visit her online at shirleyngbenitez.com.

Read More About Mei and Her Friends!

Lily's New Home

Want to Play?

Block Party

Music Time

The Garden

The Perfect Gift

Follow That Map!

The Buddy Bench

The Protest

Pablo's Pet

The Talent Show